Not

my

Girl

Not my Girl

By Caz May

My Girl duet Book 1

First Published 2020
ISBN 978-0-6488534-0-4

Published by Caz May

Author's Preface

Hey lovely readers!
Welcome to another book from my crazy mind.
This story was inspired by the song Jessie's Girl by Rick
Springfield.
And is one of my favourite tropes as well as being a rom-com
which has been a little different to write.

And a heads up lovelies there is an minor cheating part to this
story, but it's only used as a plot device. I do not condone
cheating in real life, but if this is a trigger for you may want to
look out for it towards the end of this book.

I truly hope you enjoy the story as much I enjoyed writing it.
Caz May
xx

Also by Caz May

Always Only You Series

Bk 1-Roommates Don't Kiss & Tell
Bk 2-Friends Don't Say Goodbye
Bk 3-Feelings Don't Play Fair
Bk 4-Hearts Don't Steer Us Wrong

The Mackenney Family Saga

Bk 1-Country Secrets
Bk 2-Doctor Attraction

A Holiday Romance Duet

Bk 1-Take Flight

Epigraph

Chad

You know that stupid, fucked up saying that you know when you've met the one, your soulmate who you want to spend the rest of your life with, yeah that one—well I call bull-fucking-shit on that.
It's a damn lie because I've met her —my one—but she's not my girl.

1. *Chad*

S tanding on the porch, I'm freezing my fucking balls off. It's only late March, but the temperature outside even for Melbourne is goddamn arctic.

I curse under my breath, *'come on Jessie, you fucker, open the damn door.'*

Shifting on my feet to keep warm,
I'm about to walk away from his
door when it opens. And I'm
gobsmacked by the person in front
of me. It's not my best mate, but a
fucking goddess.

I take her in, her blonde hair up in a
messy bun on her head, and her
curvaceous body in a guy's shirt.
She gives me a shy smile, biting her
lip.

"Hi, can I help you?" she purrs at
me, all seductive.

I'm fucking tongue-tied, my damn
heart pounding in my chest, and
my cock throbbing in my daks
threatening to say, *'hello'* for me
instead of my mouth.

"Um, I'm looking for Jessie."

"Oh, of course," she says with a
laugh, "he's out at the moment.
I can let him know you dropped
by."

Yeah, fat chance, honey.

The fucker knew I was coming over
and he's skipped out, leaving this
gorgeous sheila behind.

"Do you mind if I wait for him? He
was expecting me today."

"Oh, he didn't mention anything to
me or Roxanne."

Ahh, yes, Roxanne—Jessie's kid
sister—I've not seen her since she
was thirteen, and now she'd be
twenty-one.

Scratching my head I try to rack my
brain over the convo I had with
Jessie about moving in with him.
He'd mentioned roommates, but
not told me that one was a
goddess; I'd kinda guessed that one
was Roxanne though.

"Right, sure. Well, can I come in?"

The Goddess steps back from the door, ushering me in and following I stupidly glare at her, my eyes darting to her creamy thighs; the shirt lifting up to expose more to my wandering eyes.

God, she's fucking stunning.

"Would you like a coffee?" she asks, sashaying towards the kitchen after closing the front door.
I'm looking around the open-plan space, a little taken aback by the decadence of the place. But at the same time I'm not surprised Jessie Donaghey—and Roxanne—are living in such sweet digs with their parents probably paying their way through Uni.
Part of me didn't want to sponge off my loaded best mate, but after getting kicked out of Uni housing

for breaking and entering, and my subsequent breakup with Cora; short of going home with my tail between my legs, I have nowhere else to go.

I turn my attention back to the blonde goddess. "Coffee would be great."

She busies herself for a moment, using the coffee machine effortlessly. It looks like something I'd need to watch a youtube instructional video on—a hundred times—to use.

But less than a minute later, she hands me a piping hot latte.

"So, how do you know Jessie?" She asks me, sipping her own coffee.

"He's my best mate, from way back. And I need a place to crash, so here I am."

Way to go, Chad. Share ya whole damn life with this goddess when you don't even know her name.

She laughs softly, clutching her stomach. The gesture presses the thin fabric against her tits, and I gulp, nearly spitting my coffee across the room.

"So you're the elusive Chad?"

"The one and only, honey."

Get a grip man, don't call her that.

"And you are?" I ask, taking a sip of my coffee again so I don't have to meet her eyes. I'm hoping she says she's just a roommate, but a thought crashes in my mind from a couple months back; Jessie mentioning a sheila he'd met at Uni who'd knocked him for six.

And I'm clearly not going to find out right now; her reply is caught in her throat, the front door opening and my best mate walks in, smiling at us both with his cocky signature grin.

She looks at him, and her knickers clearly melt. He crosses the room, nods at me, and greets me quickly with a handshake. But his attention is not on me for much longer than a second; it's all on her. And when he gives her a soft kiss, softly saying, "Hey, baby," to her, I swear my coffee is going to come up.

She purrs back to him, "Hey to you, sexy."

They're in their own little *'make Chad chunder'* bubble, and to remind them I'm in the fucking room I clear my throat.

Thankfully they pull apart, and Jessie turns to me.

"Sorry, man. Shoulda introduced you first, or did you already exchange pleasantries?"

Inwardly I scoff, wondering who this person is; as it's not my crass best mate. He'd never say the word pleasantries.

"Well, mate, I've introduced myself to this goddess, but she didn't get the chance to introduce herself before you smashed one on her." He gives me dagger eyes, making damn sure I know I've overstepped some invisible line.

"Don't you fucking start, Chadster."

"Wasn't trying to, but you could've mentioned your girlfriend was going to be living here. Or is she not your girlfriend? Because I'll gladly take her."

"Teagan is my girlfriend, Chad. But she doesn't live here at the moment." He smiles at her, and air quotes *'at the moment'* like he's trying to prove a point.

I don't say anything to him but turn to Teagan who seems a little uncomfortable.

"Well, Teagan, nice to meet you. Sorry for being a dick."

"All good, Chadster," she replies teasingly.

Jessie clearly doesn't hear the flirtation in her tone, heading over to the coffee machine.

Teagan wraps her arms around his waist.

"I'm going to go have a shower. And leave you two to catch up."

I watch her as she leaves the room, telling my dick to stop having a party in my damn daks.

Jessie already has the shits with me, so making a move on his girl is not going to get me anywhere.

"So, Jessman, you gonna show me my new digs or what?"

He laughs; a deep chuckle.

"Only if you promise to keep ya dirty mitts of Teagan, and Roxanne."

"Roxy? She's seriously living here, with you?"

"Yes, man. And she's off limits."

"Noted, but never going to happen in this lifetime."

Jessie nods. "Then follow me, I'll show you the spare...your...room."

I follow him down the hallway; to a room at the end. Passing the bathroom, I can hear the water running from Teagan in the shower, and my dirty mind wanders to thinking of her naked and soaping up her curvaceous body.

Yep, I'm fucked, because I want Jessie's girl to be mine.

2. Roxanne

G runting, and rolling over my
hand brushes against the soft fur of
Bruno. He lets out a little growl,
self-soothing when he realises it's
me patting him.
"Morning, buddy," I greet him,
giving him a kiss on the snout.

He barks his response, jumping off my bed and padding across the floorboards to my bedroom door. He paws at it, whimpering.

Stretching, I get up, heading to the door myself.

The moment I step up behind Bruno, the cause of his whimpering is clear; voices in the hallway and one of them I've not heard in years —eight to be exact—but I know it's him.

His voice always had the power to make me giddy and giggly from my silly little girl crush on him, my brother's gorgeous as sin best friend, Chad.

Bruno lets out a bark, eager to get out of my bedroom, and most likely to also give Chad a big sloppy doggy kiss. He seemed to instantly take to Chad all those years ago and I have to admit I was kinda

jealous of the attention Chad gave
to my dog.

Opening the door a touch, I peek
out at Chad, whilst trying to stop
Bruno from bounding out to him.
My heart falls to the floor, and
butterflies go crazy in my stomach.
Chad looks even more gorgeous
than I remember, his smile wide
and his blonde hair tousled.

He elbows my brother before he
heads down the hallway and I try
to shut my door—hoping that he
didn't see me open it—but it's no
use; Bruno brushes past my legs,
rushing out the bedroom in a flurry
of fur, so eager to give Chad kisses
he jumps up on him and pushes
him against the wall.

"Hey, Bruno, you missed me huh
buddy?" Chad addresses my dog,
ruffling his head.

Bruno barks, putting his paws back on the floor and turning his head back to my door.

I'm still standing behind it, with it open just a crack. I'm trying to not hyperventilate looking at Chad, hearing his voice again. It makes me want to melt into a puddle on the floor at his feet.

"Rox, is that you?" Chad asks, using the nickname only he calls me.

To everyone else, I'm Roxy, but Chad always had to be different and always had to tease me. I knew his teasing meant nothing, he was practically a second brother but it never failed to make me weak at the knees and my heart hammer in my chest.

"Rox? I won't bite," he says again, his voice louder and closer.

I try to open my mouth, but nothing comes out.

He pushes a hand against the door, making me step back. And he takes one look at me, his eyes scanning over my body in my skimpy pyjamas before he smirks wickedly. I feel like I'm naked with his eyes on me.

"Hey Rox, you grew up," he says with a laugh.

Say something Roxy, you're not a damn mute.

I fight with my brain to tell my tongue to help me utter the words. I can't have Chad thinking I'm a tongue-tied idiot; who's got a crush on him still.

"Um, hey, Chad. So did you," I say softly, feeling like a complete fool.

So did you, what a stupid idiotic thing to say. I want to smack my own head for coming out with that.

"So did Jess tell you I'm moving in?"

"He might have mentioned it, but I...um..."

"Um, what? Thought he was pulling ya leg?"

"Yeah, I didn't think he'd be serious about torturing me."

I'm thankful my voice has decided to cooperate with me, but it hasn't stopped the butterflies in my stomach or the crazy beating of my heart. I'm sure it's loud enough for Chad to hear.

"You'll love it Rox," he teases, "Just like old times." He winks at me, and my stomach flip flops.

Just like old times. Yeah, when he'd tease me, deliberately torturing me with his good looks and playful gestures.

I'm not sure if I'm going to survive living with Chad Matthews because seeing him again, as a grown woman who knows what lust is; is already getting to me and I'm stupid to think my crush on him is long over.

"Yeah, just like old times," I reply, gulping.

He glares at me, tongue tied—for the first time ever—and it gives me a little kick. Maybe Chad is feeling something for me; now I'm all grown up.

"I'm gonna go settle into my new digs. I'll catch ya later, Rox. You might wanna put some clothes on."

Again he gives me a wink when he walks out of my bedroom, and that reaction doesn't make my stomach flip. It makes my whole body tingle.

Yep, it's confirmed, I'm still hopelessly in love with my brother's best friend.

3. Chad

*T*he rest of the day is uneventful.

I unpack my clothes, shoving them haphazardly into the drawers and hanging a few things in the wardrobe.

I don't really give a shit about stuff like that. The floor is usually my wardrobe, most of the time and the sniff test has never failed me; if it doesn't smell like b-o, shit or jizz it's good to wear again. The only thing that's going to be shit is not being able to walk around starkers or even in boxers for that matter. I'd seen the way Rox looked at me —fully clothed—her soft brown eyes drinking me in. She was practically drooling, melting into a puddle at my feet. I loved to give her a rise, knowing she had a crush on me when we were kids and by her reaction earlier it's pretty damn clear her crush still has a hold on her.

I feel sorry for her, she's not my type, although I do have to admit she's certainly grown up, now clearly showing wide fuckable hips and tits that even my hand would fail to completely grip. I'd always thought she was cute, but still, she was like a little sister and despite her having a what appears to be a bangable body I'm not going there. All day, my dick has been aching for the other beauty in the house.

The gorgeous Teagan—the fuckable blonde goddess—who I'm positive flirted with me, right in front of her boyfriend.

Jessie always was a bit daft when it came to chicks, and this isn't the first time I've lusted after a chick he's dated. But it's the first time I'm feeling so insanely jealous, that I want to hurt my best mate to get the girl.

I'm a tool, a wanker, but I can't get her off my damn mind.

I lie back on my new bed, pulling my dick out of my daks, and fisting it hard. I'm so close to coming, thinking about Teagan, but my wank is interrupted by a knock on the door.

I hear a soft intake of breath before a voice speaks softly, "Chad, pizza's here if you want some."

It's Rox, and getting up from the bed I go to the door, opening it slightly.

She's still standing there, this time dressed in trackies and a t-shirt.

"Thanks Rox. I'll be out in a jiffy. Is Teagan still here?"

"Nah, she had to head home."

"Oh, right cool. Give me a minute."

"Ok," she says with a sweet smile walking away.

I admit I take a look at her arse, and she definitely does have a pretty fine arse, but looking at it isn't making my dick spring to the party.

But the moment I think of Teagan, it's *'hello, party in Chad's daks'*.

Quickly I adjust my dick, mentally telling it to calm the fuck down and I head out of the bedroom.

Once in the kitchen I inhale the garlic and sauce smell of the pizza. And I step up behind Rox who is grabbing a piece from the boxes on the bench. She shifts uncomfortably having me so close.

I laugh, taking a piece and whispering in her ear as I step back, "Smells delicious, huh?"

She turns around, shoving her piece of Hawaiian pizza into her mouth.

"Mmm, tastes delicious to," she replies with a moan. And I swear she moans before she winks at me, grabbing another piece of pizza before heading to the lounge room.

Rox is still shy, but she seems to also have started to come out of her shell.

Maybe she isn't still crushing on me. I'll have to tease her more to find out, and bring dirty Chad out to play.

It's that or keep lusting after Jessie's girl. And I can't see that being a good idea, especially when the moment he walks out of the bathroom—and grabs a piece of pizza—he's giving me dagger eyes. But I don't want Rox. She's not my type.

4. Roxanne

All night Chad was on my mind, thoughts of how he'd touched me teasingly, and taunted me with his words.

It makes me feel a little stupid and keeping my feelings for him aside is a challenge I'm not sure I'm ready to face.

Again Bruno is eager to get out of my bedroom, pawing and barking at the door.

Opening it I peer out, looking down the hallway towards Chad's room. His door is wide open and my brothers is shut. I don't think that means anything, but I sneak out of the room, pulling the hem of my short nightie down on my thighs. My skin is covered in goosebumps, and it's not cold. I know that means Chad is near, one way my traitorous body reacts to him being nearby.

I'm about to open the bathroom door when I hear his voice, husky and panting, "Morning Rox."

I turn to find him standing next to me in the middle of the hallway; grey trackies hanging low on his hips, and shirtless, droplets of sweat dripping down the ridge of his abs.

My stomach flips, and my crotch aches, taking in his fit muscular body. He'd always had a nice body, but it's clear he's all man now and likes to keep active.

"You ok, Rox?" he asks with a smirk, gripping the t-shirt he has over his shoulder, and wiping it down his torso.

I gulp, licking my lips before I reply, "Um, yep, good. Just, um, busting."

Fuck Roxy, get a grip.

I curse myself, turning away from him to push the bathroom door open. I can feel him step up behind me, his breath in my ear.

"Don't let me stop you, but I'm dying for a shower."

Stepping in the bathroom, I'm about to shut the door behind me when Chad pushes past me.

"What the hell, Chad?"

He has the gall to laugh.

"What, Rox? I've seen you naked before."

Rolling my eyes I reply, "Yeah when I was a kid, Chad."

He laughs again, throwing his t-shirt on the floor, and slipping his trackies down his legs.

I can't stop my eyes from dropping to the front of his jocks. He has an evident bulge in them, but his dick is definitely not hard.

Again I gulp, trying to make my mouth not feel so dry. A cheeky part of me wants to yank his jocks to the floor, but I can't do that.

I'm worried he's going to do just that himself, but instead, he slides the shower curtain across, turning on the taps and stepping in before sliding it across again.

His voice comes out singsongy over the water, "You can piss now Rox; I won't hear." I can tell he's smirking with his words, and sighing I slip my knickers down my legs quickly. Putting the toilet seat down I sit on it, my elbows on my knees.

I'm hoping I don't have to also poop, as that would be embarrassment central.

My eyes glance towards the shower next to me, watching the shadow of Chad washing his body. Suddenly as I'm getting up from the toilet, he slides the curtain across a little peeking out and dropping his soaked jocks at my feet.

"What the hell, Chad?" I scream at him.

He laughs again, annoyingly.

"People usually shower naked Rox,

but I couldn't have you seeing my package."

I gulp, my mouth dry again, my tongue stuck to the roof of my mouth. Such a great time to be tongue-tied; not.

Chad is still gripping the shower curtain, smirking like a fucking devil.

"Unless you want to see my package?"

"Not a chance, Chad. It's probably a small package," I reply loudly when he pulls the curtain back to continue showering.

He calls out over the water, "Whatever you want to think Rox."

I don't reply, just pull my knickers up and open the door to slip out of the bathroom, unfortunately bumping into my brother coming out of his room.

"Morning Roxanne," he says in greeting, eyeing me questionably.

"Chad is in the bathroom," I tell him, hoping he didn't see me coming out of the bathroom when he opened his bedroom door.

"Oh right, sweet. You got class today?"

"Nah, day off. Gonna head to the beach with Nellie."

"Ok, sounds good. Catch ya later, little sis," he replies, heading down the hallway to the kitchen.

Back in my room, I flop down on my bed next to Bruno, my thoughts wandering to Chad being naked in the shower.

I wonder if I should have taunted him back more, taken him up on his offer to see his dick. But just the thought of seeing his entire birthday suit is making my knickers damp with desire, so much so I feel like shutting my door and touching myself; which I never do.

It's either that or heading back to the bathroom and getting into the shower with Chad, and the latter is a very bad idea.

5. *Chad*

*S*tanding in the kitchen, I'm staring into the fridge like it's an abyss and food is going to jump out at me. Having been for a run my stomach is grumbling with anger, something chronic.

A voice comes from behind me, followed by munching on toast, "You good, Chadster?"

"Yeah, sweet, Jessman," I reply
grinning and turning towards him
after grabbing out the two-litre
bottle of milk. There's hardly any
left, so I open the top, guzzling it
down.

Jessie laughs at me, but when I'm
about to put it down I hear another
voice, a chastising but sweet voice,
"Eww, Chad, that is seriously
gross."

Chuckling I wipe an arm across my
lips and gawk at Roxy when she
saunters into the kitchen.

She's only wearing a bikini and fuck
me does it highlight her grown-up
body.

The blue triangle bikini makes her
slightly tanned skin pop. And her
practically perfect sized tits are
pretty much escaping the top.

Of course, I'm fucking taking a look,
her body is hot and I could swear

she's deliberately flaunting this bikini to get a rise out of me.

I'm not going to give in, not going to give her that satisfaction.

Looking at Roxy practically naked still doesn't make my dick come to the party like when I think of my best mates girl, the delectable blonde goddess, Teagan.

I gulp, telling my dick to calm down from thinking about her.

She's been on my mind from the moment I met her a week or so ago. She hasn't been over though, so I've probably scared the poor chick.

Again I take a swig of the milk, gulping the remaining drops down whilst looking at Rox over the rim when I tip my head back.

It feels like I'm being stared down and swallowing the milk down hard, I chuckle, asking Jessie, "Man, why are you looking at me like I'm a wanker?"

"Because I don't like the way you're looking at my sister, Chadster."

I scoff. "And how is that Jessman?"

"Like you're thinking about something dirty."

I hear Rox's intake of breath, deep and quickly exhaled, like she can't get enough air in her lungs.

I look straight at her, and she leans over the bench to grab an apple.

"Yeah, Buckley's of that happening Jessie, relax man. I'm not after Rox."

"Keep it that way, Chad, or my fists will fuck up ya pretty boy mug."

Rox scoffs at her brothers words, and meekly but defiantly says,

"Seriously Jessie, you don't have to treat me like a damn kid."

She doesn't let her older brother reply, instead, she bites into her apple walking away from us both without another word.

"So Jessman, where's ya girl at? Did she realise you're a douche?"

"No, wanker, we're still together, but she's visiting her little sister in Brissy for a couple of weeks."

"Oh right, damn shame. Seeing her around makes for good jerk off material."

He stands up, grabbing his plate and cup and squeezing it in his grip. He's fucking irate and I step back, scared he's going to smash the glass to smithereens before walloping me over the head with it.

"You dirty fucker. You'll keep ya mitts off my sister and my girlfriend, Chad. I'm letting you stay here whilst you get back on your feet, but don't fuck up that welcome by thinking with ya dick."

"Fine, Jessie. But anyone other than them is fair game," I call out heading down the hallway to grab my surfboard.

Rox is in her room, texting on her phone when I pass her door.

"Rox, you mind if I tag along to the beach?"

She looks up at me, trying to hide her grin.

"Um, yeah sure. Mind riding with me and coming to pick up my friend?"

"Will she be wearing a bikini?"

"I don't know, Chad," she snaps at me.

"Doesn't matter. You look good in yours, Rox."

"Don't Chad, ok. Just get your stuff, and meet me outside."

She walks out, brushing past me and jumping back like I gave her an electric shock on steroids.

She's got it bad for me, I'm sure of it and for some reason unbeknownst to myself I want to tease Rox.

Making her squirm is fun, even if it's a bad idea.

6. Roxanne

The entire trip to the beach I had to endure Chad giving Nellie side-eye glances into the back seat of my Jeep. The way she was looking at him—at my Chad—made my stomach knot up.

Granted she doesn't know how I feel about him, but I'm sure she knows who he is and that should be enough for her to steer clear. The moment I pull up at Williamstown beach, Chad is out of the car, grabbing his surfboard from the back and he's sprinting down the beach without glancing back at us or even saying a word. Anyone would think he's wound up tighter than a spring; like I am. Nellie gets out, grabbing her backpack and throwing it over her shoulder.

I lock the Jeep and follow her down onto the sand. Finding a spot to sit, we kick off our thongs and lay down our beach towels before sitting down on them.

She bites down on her lip, her gaze focusing on the water when she says, "So give me the goss, Roxy?"

"What goss?" I reply laughing and turning to look at my best friend when I pull my sundress over my head.

"The goss with you and the delicious specimen out there surfing like he owns the sea."

"No goss to tell, Nel."

"Bullshit, Roxy. You could barely stop gawking at him in the car."

"I was doing nothing of the sort, Nel. I was driving."

"And looking at him out of the corner of your eyes."

"Fine, you got me, but there's nothing to tell."

"Right, so you just picked up some random gorgeous as fuck hottie to come to the beach with us?"

"No, dufus. He's my brother's best friend in case you've forgotten and is living with us for a while."

Nellie gapes at me. "He's living with you, and you haven't jumped him?"

"No, Nel. Did you not hear me say brothers best friend? Jessie would kill us both."

"Yeah, but fuck Roxy. I'd take the damn risk."

I don't reply, instead lick my lips, looking towards the water where Chad is riding a wave into shore. He looks absolutely gorgeous—in his element—the wetsuit clinging to his sculpted body, practically one with his own skin. He starts to walk up the beach, and Nel laughs at me, looking over and laughing whilst touching her face at the corner of her mouth.

"You got a little drool there, Roxy."

I elbow her in the side. "Stop it, Nel! And don't get any ideas about Chad. He's off-limits."

"Noted, but a little harmless flirting never hurt anyone," she replies with a laugh, gulping when Chad stops in front of us, digging the end of his surfboard into the sand and leaning against it; with a wicked tantalising smirk on his face.

It highlights his lickable double dimple on the left side of his face, and I bite my lip, pondering standing up and kissing the smirk right off his face; which of course I can't do.

He looks at Nellie, and laces his tone with flirtation, "So, I didn't get to introduce myself in the car, gorgeous. I'm Chad."

Nellie bounces up, her boobs bouncing with her—practically in Chad's face—and she gives him a giggly smile.

"Nellie. Nice to meet you Chad."

"Oh, likewise Nellie. I couldn't help but stare at you whilst I was out surfing." His eyes don't meet hers but drop to her boobs, and the traitor doesn't care one bit.

Her own gaze travels down his body to the impressive package at the front. And I scoff, standing up and collecting our things from the sand.

They're eye-fucking each other and I feel like chundering. I know Chad is only doing it to get a rise out of me, but I'm not taking his bait.

"Are you two going to stand there and eye fuck each other all day or can we go home now?"

Chad turns to look at me, teasing, "Is someone jelly, Rox?"

"No," I snap, my eyes darting from him to Nellie who's giving me a questioning look from the nickname Chad called me.

She's mouthing it to me and I shrug, a non-verbal warning to tell her to keep her mouth shut.

"I just want to go home."

"Whatever you say, Rox, but I'm driving this time. You drive like a damn snail."

We all walk up the beach and I throw Chad the keys, getting in the front seat when he unlocks the doors.

Nellie whispers in my ear from the seat behind, "You're a liar, Rox. There is so something going on with you two."

I huff, turning back to look at her when Chad gets in the jeep.

"I'll tell you later."

She doesn't reply and we pull into the afternoon traffic.

The car is silent and the tension is eating at me, all the way to Nellie's house.

7. Chad

A fter the beach, and dropping Nellie off there's a weird tension in the car.

I can tell Rox is pissed off with me and it's probably because I cracked onto Nellie right in front of her.

Her jeep is an automatic, super easy to drive, so I punch her in the arm teasing her, "So Rox, were you jelly watching me crack onto Nellie?"

"No, of course, I wasn't," she snaps at me, blushing a deep crimson.

"Come on Rox, don't give me that bullshit. You want me."

"I don't want you Chad," she spits at me, turning away to look out the window and to hide her even deeper blush. She'd shut me down but I'm not so sure she's telling me the truth.

I feel kinda bad for teasing her, so ask, "You'd tell me if ya loved me Rox, yeah?"

I touch her arm and she turns to look at me when she replies, "Of course, and in your dreams Chad." She practically purrs my name, making it clear that she's got feelings for me.

I'm guessing she's liked me for a long time; since we were kids and

I'd practically spent every weekend at the Donaghey's house whilst my parents were off overseas pretending to be the most amazing missionaries.

All they'd really done was spend every cent they earnt on anything but their children. It makes me feel like a bad son, but I don't miss them, and I don't even remember shedding a tear at their funeral either.

The only legacy they left me with is a mega fear of flying, having died in a plane crash coming home from the Philippines.

Once inside the house, I run towards the bathroom, calling out, "Dibs on the shower, Rox."
She follows behind me, huffing and walking slowly. I can feel her eyes

on me, watching as I'm stripping off whilst I walk down the hallway.

It's careless, and daring but I don't close the door straight away; deliberately.

I start pulling my boardies down facing forward towards the open door.

From the hallway, I hear Rox outside the door. She lets out a loud gulp, a whimper of sorts when my boardies drop to the floor.

Her reaction to seeing me naked is an ego boost for sure; not that I need one.

Rox heads back down the hallway and I laugh, kicking the door shut before getting in the shower.

Starting to soap up my body, my thoughts wander to her; the girl I can't have, Jessie's girl Teagan. And my dick is instantly hard.

8. Roxanne

S cooting back to my room after
seeing Chad naked, I'm cursing
myself for looking at him. My heart
is hammering in my chest, and I
can't stop thinking about how
glorious his body is.

I know for certain now that his dick
is not small at all. And I'm no

expert on male anatomy, but his dick looked damn good; good enough to eat.

I close my door, and lie down on my bed, listening to him in the shower.

He's singing loudly and he's good just like I remembered from when we were kids singing karaoke; his voice melodic and has a deep baritone sound to it.

I don't know what he's singing, but it makes me feel giddy and stirs up the butterflies in my belly, as well as sending that rush to my nether region.

Striping from my bikini I lower my hand to my crotch, starting to play with myself by flicking a finger over my clit.

Thinking about him naked—seeing him naked—has made me so wet and I can't help but imagine I'm in the shower with him and making him moan.

The pleasure is intense and I close my eyes, just for a moment.

My moans are loud, I can't hold them in and I'm about to come when I realise the water has stopped and someone is knocking on my bedroom door.

My hand is still on my crotch and I freeze hearing his voice.

"Rox, you ok in there?" he asks with a tone that suggests he's smirking.

"Um, yep, good...um...fuck...yep," I yell out in reply, my traitorous body coming at the same time in a rush.

"Rox?" Chad asks again, sounding more concerned this time, opening my door and stumbling into my bedroom.

He looks at me on the bed, holding back a laugh, but not able to hide his smirk and delectable dimples. "Seriously Chad, get out!" I scream at him, stumbling to my feet and wrapping the sheet around my naked body; hoping he didn't see anything.

"Why Rox? Are you naked?" he taunts, taking a few steps further into my room.

"Yes, I'm naked and I'm…um…well, I was um…busy."

He laughs, deep, before teasing me, "Oh Roxanne, you dirty girl. Were you flicking ya bean?"

Stumbling towards him I blurt out, "No…just get out of my room Chad."

I feel a blush rise up my cheeks.

"Oh you so were Rox," he jeers, turning away to walk out.

He lets his towel drop to the floor, giving me a view of his perfectly round arse when he taunts, "And I know you saw my dick, so you're welcome."

I scoff, picking up his discarded towel and throwing at him.

He grabs it and heads out of my bedroom; wiggling his arse at me.

I flop back down on my bed, sighing and cursing myself for giving into how he makes me feel.

I might as well tattoo, *'I love Chad Matthews'* on my forehead.

I'm sure he knows how I feel but clearly doesn't feel the same back.

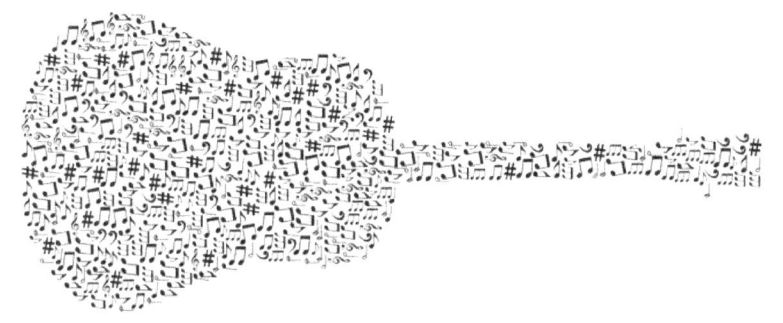

9. Chad

*T*hrashing my arms about I wake up with a start, dripping wet from a cold sweat.

For the life of me, I can't fucking remember what the fuck I was dreaming about.

Getting up and stumbling to the door, I'm shocked and annoyed to find Rox standing outside my bedroom door.

"What do you want Rox?" I ask, hoping my tone sounds pissed off because I am.

"Are you ok? You were screaming."

"Um, yep I'm fine," I mutter, gulping hard.

She's standing in front of me, completely dumbstruck, staring at my body and lapping up my half nakedness like a damn puppy. Thankfully I wore grey trackies to bed last night, or she'd be getting the full package view again.

I push her inside my bedroom, sliding her light body against the wall.

Her breath hitches when I pin her against the wall, standing in front of her so she can't move.

"Did I say anything? You know in my sleep?" I ask feeling panicked, worried that I'd said something about Teagan in my crazy dreams. I'd been known to sleep talk, but it hadn't happened in years.

My body reacts to thoughts of Teagan crashing into my mind, my dick tenting my trackies so much that I have to jut my arse out so it's not against Rox's pelvis.

"Um...yeah...you said...." Rox starts telling me something but I cut her off with a finger against her lips. "Actually Rox, don't tell me," I tell her with a chuckle that I'm really not feeling.

I kinda do want to know if I said something, but I don't know if Rox is playing me, or if she'd tell me the truth. She always made up stories when we were kids, and I pretended to love them, even when I thought they were stupid, fanciful and childish.

Rox huffs and I step back leaving her standing against my bedroom wall.

I walk out of the bedroom, and heading past the bathroom I can hear the running shower, so instead of barging in I head straight to the kitchen and find Teagan there cooking breakfast.

Her hair is up in one of those messy buns on her head, and she's wearing what is clearly one of Jessie's t-shirts. It barely covers her arse and fuck it's a damn turn on.

I step up behind her, moaning into her ear with a salacious whisper, "Mmm...smells delicious. And looks fucking delectable." My words are a tease, not related to the food, but her and being so close to her delectable body.

She turns around and her aforementioned body is right in my

personal space, pressed up against the fatty in my trackies.

Her chest rises, and all I can think about is crashing my lips to hers, but she breaks the moment I'm sure we're having by speaking, "Yeah, pancakes are my speciality." She's waving the spatula in her hand, and smirking at me.

Fuck this chick is gonna kill me.

"Oh, I bet they are," I purr into her ear.

She huffs at me, putting her hands against my bare abs. And I groan at the contact. It makes my whole body throb, including my dick that wants to take her hard against the kitchen counter.

"So if you don't mind I'd like to get back to cooking them," she says sweetly and clearly rhetorical but I bite back.

"Oh, I mind, Teagan," I tease grabbing her arse cheek in my grip when she turns back around.

She giggles, but slaps my hand away when Jessie walks in.

He gives me dagger eyes, and if looks could kill I'd probably be a dead man.

"Morning Chadster," he says with an odd almost angry tone in his voice.

I step away from Teagan to greet my best mate. "Morning Jessie," I spit, stupidly pissed off for his appearance in the kitchen.

Jessie walks past me when I bend down to get the milk out of the fridge for a coffee.

He seethes in my ear, "I'll cut ya fucking hand off if you touch her again."

I turn to face him, getting all up in his face when I sneer, "Yeah right Jessman. You'd never hurt me, brother. Don't you faint at the sight of blood?"

Teagan's eyes are like saucers, watching us both, whilst holding up a plate of pancakes.

She's clearly enjoying this verbal spat between Jessie and me.

"No, that's you Chad, you always were a wuss."

I don't reply, just watch—and try not to chunder— when Jessie kisses Teagan softly on the lips. My stomach turns when he purrs to her, "Good morning baby."

Jealousy hits me hard in the chest and I curse myself for the feelings I shouldn't be having. I'm jealous as hell and turned on.

The only thing I can do is head to the shower and wank thinking of her being mine and not Jessie's girl.

10. Roxanne

S itting on the couch, watching a movie with Jessie and Teagan I'm bored as. The movie is beyond lame, some stupid thriller, with a weird romance plot underneath it all. I don't really want to go to my room, so instead, I get up heading to the kitchen with a skip to make popcorn.

Grabbing out the popping corn and a pot I laugh to myself when I get out the butter, thinking about making popcorn when I was younger. Chad always made it, slathering it in enough butter to give you a heart attack.

Speaking of the devil himself he saunters into the kitchen, coming up behind me when I shake the hot pan.

"Hey Rox," he greets me happily, stepping closer and teasing me, "Mmm, Rox are you trying to butter me up."

His tone is husky, and I swear I hear him gulp. I turn towards him, taking in a deep breath to make sure I don't stay something stupid.

"No, I'm just making popcorn."

He chuckles, deep, making his chest that is way to close to mine vibrate and I have to take in a deep breath, to not hyperventilate.

"I can see that, Rox. Something up with you?" he asks, giving me a smirk, but his eyes show concern.

"No, nothing, I'm fine," I stammer, trying to sound calm.

Again he laughs, taking a step back, thankfully.

"So you're putting extra butter on the popcorn for another guy?" he taunts, poking me in the chest, under my boobs.

"Um...no I like extra butter."

"Right sure you do Rox. Or you're making it how I used to make it when we were kids?"

I start to walk away, not able to meet his eyes that are staring at me oddly.

"I don't know what you're talking about," I snap handing him the bowl full of popcorn when we head back to the lounge room.

Teagan and Jessie are on one of the two-seater couches snuggled together under the throw rug.

I don't even want to know what their hands are doing underneath the throw where I can't see them.

Chad plonks himself down on the other couch, laughing at me when I sit on the floor, putting the popcorn on the coffee table.

"Rox, I don't bite, I promise. Get ya butt up here," he jeers, his signature smirk plastered on his face.

I don't know whether to trust him. His teasing lately has been full-on, and I don't know how he's feeling about me.

Shrugging, I stand up and sit on the couch on the other side, away from Chad. He chuckles and pulls me closer, putting my feet in his lap. My eyes dart towards his crotch and I can see why he wanted me closer. His eyes are focused on Teagan and Jessie watching the movie. They're giving each other sweet kisses and it's clear that Chad isn't watching the movie. Chad's dick is hard.

My mind wanders to whether I could make it hard, but I'm sure that's probably just wishful thinking. He's seen me practically naked and his dick stayed flaccid. I shove popcorn into my mouth to try and not laugh at the fact that he's getting turned on by watching my brother kissing his girlfriend. Suddenly I feel Chad's dick throb against the balls of my feet and I choke on the popcorn I just shoved into my mouth.

Chad's attention turns to me, and he asks, "You ok Rox?"

"Yep...popcorn went down the wrong way," I reply, gasping and jumping off the couch to run and get a glass of water.

11. *Chad*

F ollowing Rox into the kitchen,
she jumps back from the fridge,
nearly dropping the bottle of water
she's holding on the floor.
"Fuck Chad," she curses, "you
scared the bejesus out of me."
She unscrews the lid and takes a
big gulp of the water. A drop lingers

on her lip, and she licks it. I must admit it's kinda hot.

"Sorry, Rox. I didn't mean to scare you, but I had to get out of there."

Her eyes light up. "Huh? Why?" she replies with a laugh.

"Watching them kissing makes me feel like chundering but also well... you know," I say nodding towards my crotch.

Again she laughs and replies, "Oh, I know Chad. I felt it and I..."

She gulps down some more water, practically moaning when she swallows it.

"And what Rox?" I ask confused.

She finishes gulping down her water and shaking her head she mutters, "Oh nothing...forget about it. I'm going to bed."

I know I shouldn't ask what I'm about to, but I'm not tired and don't really want to spend another moment watching Jessie and Teagan together. I'd not be able to keep my dinner down or my dick down either.

"Want some company?"

"Um...no," Rox snaps back, blushing.

"You have a tv in your room, don't you?" I ask.

She doesn't give me an answer, just throws her water bottle in the recycling bin and starts to walk away.

"Maybe we could watch a movie together instead?" I ask her again.

"What? Like old times?"

"Yeah, come on Rox...I miss those moments."

She huffs at me, folding her arms across her chest.

"Fine...but no funny business...and you can't get under the covers with me."

"Deal," I agree, following her to her bedroom and plonking myself down on her double bed; flicking on the tv.

She doesn't get into bed, instead trudges into her walk-in wardrobe, calling out to me, "Choose a movie, I'm just going to put some PJ's on."

Opening Netflix I scroll through the new movies, choosing a thriller.

Rox comes out of the wardrobe in a nightie that dips at her cleavage and is high on her thigh.

It's pretty damn sexy looking and I wonder if she's after more than just watching a movie, in bed, with an old friend.

"Damn Rox...you trying to impress me?"

"No," she says defensively, stepping closer to her bed, "I love this nightie. It's comfy."

I shake my head, trying to clear my head of thoughts about what she might have underneath.

I'm not attracted to Rox—at least I think I'm not—but she's got a damn good body and I'm a guy. Nothing more needs to be said, but I find myself asking, "Right, and are you wearing undies under it? A bra?

"No…just a g-string," she replies, climbing onto the bed; pulling back the covers

She's about to get under the covers when I slap her arse, lifting the nightie up to check out her arse. And damn, I've gotta admit Rox has a ripper arse; pert and smooth.

"Chad…don't," Rox protests through giggles.

"Sorry was just checking that you weren't fibbing," I reply with a

smirk when she sits down and pulls
the covers up over her body.

I don't dare look at her tits, as I'm
sure they're probably standing to
attention and the thought of
turning her on admittedly gets me
a little excited myself.

"Just put the movie on," she tells
me, not daring to look at me, her
eyes focusing only on the TV.

"Fine but can I get comfy first?"

"Um yeah, I guess...depends I
guess," she mutters, looking at me
out of the corner of her eyes.

I don't reply, just stand up and yank
off my jeans and t-shirt, leaving
only my boxers on.

Getting back onto the bed I press
play and Roxy snuggles against me,
resting her head on my shoulder.

I whisper in her ear, "See just like
old times."

She mutters an, *'mmm'* in response, blushing.

I can't concentrate on the movie, my mind wandering to Teagan and Jessie in the next room, and for a moment I wish it was me with Teagan, pashing on the couch.

But what scares me the most is that for a moment I wish that I could have that with Rox, because it's clear she wants that with me. But she's not my girl. Neither of them are. And neither of them can be. Jessie would kill me either way, and no girl is worth getting my arse kicked for.

12. Roxanne

*R*olling over in bed waking up the next day, I'm both shocked and relieved to find myself alone; except for Bruno at my feet. He'd obviously come in sometime during the night.

I remember watching a movie with Chad and falling asleep, but he's

not in my bed anymore so I'm
wondering if I dreamt it.
He'd let me lean on his shoulder,
and he was half-naked, wearing
only tight red boxer shorts that
didn't hide his glorious dick.
He didn't know that just having him
that close had made my g-string a
piece of damp fabric.
I'm not sure I even want to face
him, so getting out of bed I tiptoe
down the hallway to the bathroom
to brush my teeth and hair.
I'd made plans to go out for coffee
with Nellie.

After quickly getting ready and
letting Bruno out into the backyard,
I sneak out, so to not wake Chad or
my brother and head to the tram to
go to the new coffee shop Nellie
told me about.

It's a short trip, and Nellie is waiting outside when I arrive. Walking up to her, she wraps me in a friendly hug.

"Hey girl, what's with the tomboy look?"

"Nothing. Trackies are comfy, that's all."

"You could make more of an effort, Roxy."

"Whatever, Nel. Let's just go in and grab a drink. It's freezing out here."

"Yeah, damn right. I'm freezing my damn tits off." I laugh at her, following her inside the coffee shop.

"You don't have tits to freeze off, Nel," I tease.

"Yeah, true. Do you still want an iced coffee?"

"Nah, I'm thinking a cappuccino might be in order."

We sit down on some rather comfy looking couches a few minutes later with our coffee's in hand.

I take a sip of mine, sighing deeply when I put it down on the table in front of us.

"So, did you jump him yet?"

"What? Who?" I ask, feigning shock, because I know she's talking about Chad.

"Your roommate, dufus."

"Oh…um, no. I haven't jumped Chad."

"And why the fuck not? He's damn hot Roxy. I'd have climbed him like a tree if he was my roommate."

"He doesn't like me that way, Nell. And he made that clear as blazers last night."

She gives me a questioning look. "Yeah, how so?"

"We watched a movie together…in my bed."

"Ooo, so you snuggled?"

"Yeah, but it wasn't like that. He stayed on top of the covers and didn't make a move, even though he was only in his boxers."

"You could have though, Roxy," she chastises me.

I sigh, taking a deep breath in.

"I know, but I thought he was going to after he slapped me on the arse teasingly, but straight after that he went back into big brother mode like when we were kids and he lived with us."

Nellie gapes at me, shocked words rolling off her tongue at warp speed, "He lived with you before? Like when? Seriously? Fuck Roxy!"

"Yeah, he used to stay over a lot when his parents were away overseas, and when they died he lived with us for a while before he went into a foster care house with his little sister Carly."

"Oh my gosh, Roxy. So I'm guessing you've always had the hots for him then?"

I grab my coffee gulping it down and muttering, "It's more than that Nel. I'm in love with him."

Nellie replies with a slight laugh, "I knew it. And what are you going to do about your undeniable love for Chad?"

I laugh, spitting the last mouthful of my coffee out.

"Absolutely nothing. He doesn't feel that way about me."

Shaking her head at me, she chastises me again, "Well, do something to make him see you that way."

"Like what?" I ask, feeling stupid and a lot more innocent than I am.

"I don't know...tease him. Flaunt your curves baby," Nellie suggests with a laugh.

"Yeah, I guess. But I can't exactly prance around the house in my underwear."

"Yeah, I know that dufus. You need to show him what he's missing though."

"Hmm, yeah. I'll think about it," I reply, giving my best friend a shy smile.

"We should go out together," she suddenly blurts out, a little to eager, "get tanked."

I laugh and reply, "It's his birthday in a week or so."

"Perfect...drag his arse out and get tanked together," Nellie suggests excitedly with a cheeky smile.

"All right," I reply softly before adding, "and Nel I'm sorry."

"What for?"

"Being in love with him and getting jealous when he cracked onto you. I know you like him to."

"Forget it, Roxy...he's yours," she tells me happily, but then adds cheekily with a hint of malice, "you lucky bitch."

I laugh her snide remark off and stand up to pull her into a hug.

"Anyway, girl, I gotta scoot to work. Text me the plans for Chadster's birthday and we can work out your outfit via FaceTime or something."

"Will do," I reply laughing inwardly at her calling him 'Chadster'.

Nellie leaves and my mind wanders to ideas of what to do for Chad's birthday.

Heading back out of the coffee shop I think back to the silly karaoke parties I made him do with me when we were kids. And one particular one when I was about thirteen flashes in my mind. It wasn't long before Chad left to live in the Foster house.

❤

I'm clutching the microphone in a fist, waiting for the song to start on my Disney sing party PlayStation game. Other than the sounds from the TV, the rumpus room and the whole house is super quiet.

I don't feel like such a dufus in a quiet house when 'A whole new world' starts playing.

The male part taps out and I'm ready for the female part, blurting it out at the top of my lungs when I feel Chad come into the rumpus room.

I can always sense his presence, by the goosebumps that erupt over every inch of my skin.

The male part is on again, and Chad joins in singing the words perfectly. He grabs me around the waist, teasing me by swaying our hips together.

It makes me feel tingly all over and when the song ends and he steps back I feel like I can't breathe.

"You were good Rox. Can I choose a song to sing?"

"Um, yeah. They're all Disney songs though."

"All good. Disney songs rock my socks off, Rox."

I laugh at his stupid words, watching him scroll through the list of songs. My heart skips when he chooses to put on 'kiss the girl'.

He starts singing it in his deep voice, and I feel like melting into a puddle at his feet. He's singing it to me, not looking at the screen but at me, and he's standing close enough to actually kiss me. But I can't let that happen, so in a panic, a rush of shyness takes over and I run out of the room and straight upstairs to my bedroom, still listening to Chad finishing the song. Slamming the door behind me I let the tears fall down my cheeks. I wanted to kiss 'Chad Matthews', my brother's best friend.

❤

Even now, ten years later that memory still gets to me, but I know without a doubt that taking Chad out for drunken karaoke on his birthday is the best idea.
I'm giddy with excitement, and I hope that it might just get Chad to see me as more than Jessie's little sister.

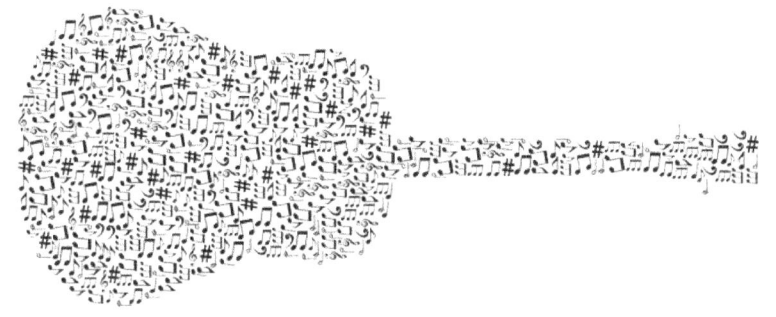

13. *Chad*

*S*ince the night I'd spent in Rox's room a couple of weeks ago, we'd been tiptoeing around each other, not talking much at all except for the occasional muttering groans of a *'good morning'.* And I hate admitting to myself that I'm missing spending time with her; missing riling her up.

Everything else in my life at this point has been a complete downer, making me feel like a complete useless failure.

I know I should be happy I've got a job, even though it's a shitty barman job and I always have to work the day shift when all the drunk old men are in ordering countless pots of beer. And the other downer is not being at Uni anymore, as not using my brain to focus on my structural engineering degree makes me feel like I'm in a black hole. I never was good enough for my parents, and even though they're not around anymore to see my failures I still feel like they're berating me for my shortcomings.

Walking in the house after work I honestly just want to crawl into bed and sleep off the hangover feeling that's plaguing me from another day in my shitty job.

The smell of all the alcohol—on an empty stomach—always gives me a raging headache.

I'm about to head straight to the comfort of my bed when I hear a groan of pain coming from the lounge room.

Heading there I find Roxy is on the couch, sick, shivering from fever and with a bucket beside her on the floor.

Stepping up closer to the couch and standing by her feet hanging out of the throw rug over her body I ask, "Rox you ok?"

She sits up a little, clutching the throw rug against her chest. "Do I look ok, Chad?" she snaps at me, grunting her annoyance.

"No," I reply chuckling and bending down beside the couch; touching a hand to her forehead.

"Fuck, Rox, you're burning up," I curse loudly pulling my hand back and shaking it.

"I'm freezing Chad," she says, a shiver rushing through her body, "and my head hurts and my stomach aches."

Standing up, I offer, "I'm going to run you a bath."

Rox blushes, and says meekly, "But I have to be naked for that."

Again I chuckle at her innocent response. "Just leave ya knickers and bra on, Rox," I suggest with a teasing hint in my tone.

She murmurs a meek, "ok."

"Can you walk?" I ask reaching out my hand to pull the throw rug off her.

"Yeah, I'm not a cripple, Chad," she replies with a snigger.

She sits up, and curses out a loud, "Fuck!"

"What?" I plead worriedly.

"I feel dizzy. The whole room is spinning," she informs me, falling back down onto her arse on the couch.

I grab her around the waist, helping her stand up and she falls against me, weak in my arms.

Scooping her up into my arms— bridal style—I carry her towards the bathroom.

Putting her down, I hold her against my side and close the door before awkwardly bending down to turn on the bath tap.

She's shivering in my arms, and it breaks my cold heart seeing her in pain. Gripping her hip with one hand, and with the other, I lift up her t-shirt to pull it off. It makes a memory flash in my mind.

❤

Watching Rox run around the backyard I can't help but laugh from the tree I'm standing behind whilst we're playing hide and seek. She's deliberately looking in all the wrong spots, running around and calling out, "Chaddy, come out, come out wh…" her words are cut off by her almost bloodcurdling scream.

Rushing out from behind the tree I'm hiding behind, I find Rox sitting on the grass clutching her knee and crying in agony. Her pretty pale pink dress is slashed open at the front and stained with blood.

My heart catches in my throat, my eyes gawking around for what could have caused the gash across her stomach.

Reaching her I soothe her, "Rox, it's ok. Tell me what happened."

She sniffs back tears, muttering, "I...I...was...running...and I...tripped on...the edge...of the oncrete."

She's hiccuping now, and still sobbing.

"Show me where it hurts?" I ask, prying her hands away from her knee. There's a scrap there, with blood trickling out. "And your belly?"

She points beside her on the concrete, at the sharp stick lying there.

Picking it up I ask, "Did this cut you?"

"Yeah...and it hurts."

"Yeah, let's get you inside. And we can call your Mum."

"Ok, but don't tell Jessie I got hurt whilst we were playing. He won't let me play with you when you come over if you do."

Her words are so matter of fact— now she's not sobbing—and leaning into my side, a hand wrapped around her back we hobble inside to the downstairs bathroom.

I can hear some music playing from the rumpus room, so it seems like Jessie is otherwise preoccupied with playing Rock band on Playstation. It's all he ever does these days, whenever I'm over and I'd honestly rather play outside with Rox, even if an eleven-year-old boy playing with an eight-year-old girl is weird. I like her company, and like to tease her.

Sitting her down on the edge of the bath, I grab a face washer, wetting it and pressing a pump of the vanilla hand soap onto it, before I wipe over her knee gently.

She hisses at the contact.

"That stings, Chad."

"I know Rox, but I have to clean it first."

"Before you can put a Minnie mouse bandaid on it?"

"Yeah, exactly Rox. Now show me the cut on your belly?" Her cheeks turn red, like a tomato, and I poke her softly.

"What's wrong, Rox? I'm just trying to help."

"I know, but Mummy told me I shouldn't get nakie in front of other people."

I'm about to reply when she adds, "especially boys."

"I'm not just any boy Rox. I won't hurt you, and you're like my little sister."

"Yeah," she mutters with a huff, letting me lift the dress over her head with her arms up.

Throwing it on the floor, I stumble back when I hear a bellowing voice behind me, "What the hell are you doing to my sister?"

Standing up I stammer, "Nothing Jessie, she fell over outside whilst we were playing and I was just cleaning up her cuts."

"You should have gone to get Mum. She's only next door at the Goodman's."

"I know, I'm sorry, but I just wanted to help."

"Whatever, Chad, get out, and go and get Mum," my best friend

shouts at me, pushing me out the bathroom door.

Walking out I look at Rox who is sobbing again, with Jessie rubbing the face washer over the deep cut on her stomach.

It looks really bad, and I swallow down the lump in my throat from worry running out the front door to the neighbours.

❤

"Chad?" her voice asks softly.

"Yeah, Rox?"

"Can I get in now? And why are you looking at me like that?"

I shake my head, turning my gaze back to her face and away from the light scar on her stomach.

"Sorry, Rox, I was just thinking about the day you got this scar," I tell her running my finger delicately across her skin as I help her into the bath.

She laughs softly. "Oh yeah, Jessie was so pissed off."

"Yeah, he'd never been that angry with me."

"I liked you helping me. Same now."

I don't reply, instead just hand her a face washer to run over her heated skin.

I can't help but let my eyes wander over her body—even though she's still wearing underwear—I can see her nipples screaming through her crop bra. Her tits are practically falling out of it, and I have to resist the temptation to grab them in my hands to warm her up—no wait, cool her down—that's what you need to do for a fever, *you fucking idiot.*

"You can leave me be Chad. I'll be fine. I kinda want to take off my underwear."

"Fine, but I'm just going to turn around, and you can close the curtain."

"Ok, big brother," she teases with a laugh. And I hate admitting to myself that those words punch me in the guts.

I don't want to be her big brother. I don't know what I want from Rox, but it sure as hell isn't big brother status. She's got one of those, and even though I'm staying in his house at the moment I'm not his fave person.

Facing the other side of the room, I shriek in shock when a pair of plain white wet cotton undies and a matching crop bra are dropped beside me. And I hear Rox's voice, "Payback, Chad."

I chuckle, a smirk on my face when dirty thoughts flash into my mind— thoughts of pulling the curtain back and checking her out; naked—but it's Rox behind there and even thinking about her naked isn't even making my dick a little hard.

It only says hello when thoughts of a blonde chick come to mind—*oh fucking grea*t—now I'm hard.

Awkwardly, I stand up, grabbing a towel and turning back around to face the bathtub.

"Rox, are you done?"

"Yeah, just letting the water out. Can you grab me a towel?"

I slide the curtain back—closing my eyes—and hand her the towel.

"You can look now," she tells me, and I open my eyes, gulping when I take her hand to help her step out of the bath. She looks good in a towel, but Teagan would look better my head reminds me; my dick following suit.

Walking out into the hallway, I'm heading to my room when Rox asks, "Can you lie with me? Until I fall asleep."

"Yeah, if you want," I reply, following her into her bedroom. She slips her nightie over her body and lets the towel drop to the floor. And getting into the bed beside her —she snuggles into my chest—and I know this is most definitely a very bad idea.

I don't make good choices when it comes to Roxanne, and I know that Jessie is going to have my head if he finds out I'm again taking care of his kid sister.

I shouldn't feel like I need to take care of her. Rox is not my girl, but still, I soothe her, smoothing the hair off her forehead, and I smile when she says sleepily, "Thanks for taking care of me, Chad."

"Anytime, Rox," I reply closing my eyes even though I shouldn't.

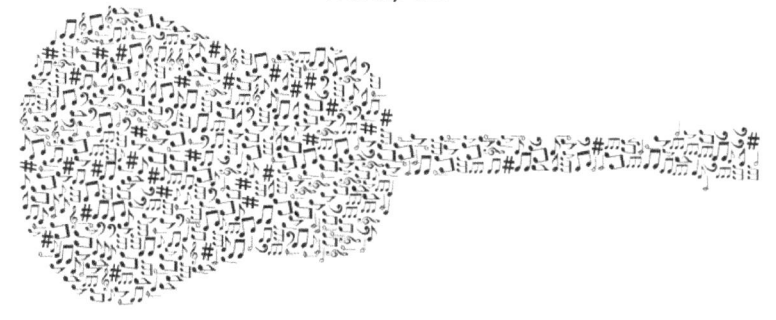

14. *Chad*

*R*olling over, waking up, my arm feels like a dead weight. I'm fucking holding Rox in my arms. She's still sleeping, soft moans escaping her lips. It's kinda cute. I don't want to disturb her, but it's clear I need to get out of her bed right fucking now; my dick is hard. I can't believe I'm in a bed—with Rox—and my goddamn dick has decided to have a party in my daks. I'm thinking maybe I dreamt of Teagan, and this morning hard-on is because of that, not the fact that Rox's pert, non-covered arse is pressing up against my crotch. But of course, I'm panicking, thinking about what Rox will think if she wakes up and finds me one, still in her bed, and two, with a damn hard on.

Slowly, so I don't wake her I peel my arm away from her side, edging away from her body before flinging my legs over the side of the bed. I rush out of her room and back to mine, flopping down on the bed. Closing my eyes, I slide a hand into my boxers and fist my dick, stroking it with thoughts of Teagan filling my mind.

After what seems like hours I wake up again, still with a hard-on. I think of all matter of rotten things to calm it down and climb out of bed, heading to the kitchen to get some brekky into my grumbling guts. Sauntering into the kitchen, in only my boxers I find Rox making breakfast; bacon and eggs which smells divine. Inhaling the smell my guts grumble more, and I step up behind her, teasingly pressing my dick against her arse. She wiggles a little and whimpers in an odd sexy kinda way.

It makes me shift backwards, with a smirk on my face that I can't hide even though I want to when Rox turns around smiling at me.

"Thanks for looking after me last night," she says sweetly.

"No worries, Rox. I'm sorry for this morning though," I say gruffly.

"This morning? What happened this morning?"

"Um...oh nothing...just not waking up in your bed. Thought you might have missed me," I jeer, stepping up closer to her again, and grabbing her around the waist to tickle her like I used when we were kids.

"Stop, Chad, stop," she protests, squirming in my arms and giggling. Letting her go, I smirk at her again, feeling an odd rush of emotions hit me. It's not the intense physical attraction I feel for Teagan, but something else entirely and it's scary as hell because this is Rox—Roxanne, my surrogate little sister—that I'm thinking about.

In my daze, I don't realise she's turned around again to finish the bacon and eggs.

To her back I ask, "Is something bothering you Rox?"

She laughs, turning around with a plate of greasy brekky goodness.

"Yeah, I wanted to ask you something."

"Oh? If it's a date then it's a no."

"Of course it's not asking you on a date."

"Then what, Rox?" I jeer, nabbing a piece of the bacon and biting down on it hard.

"I was thinking we should all go out for your birthday, drinks and karaoke."

"Sounds ripper, Rox. Give me the deets and I'm so there," I reply, nabbing another piece of bacon and heading back to my bedroom.

15. Roxanne

*P*utting my MacBook up on my dresser I open FaceTime and dial Nellie. Her smiling face pops up on my screen. "Hey girl, please tell me you're going to wear those?"

Laughing I glance down at my black bra and g-string, that barely cover any skin and make my boobs pop. "Oh, yeah, totally. But sadly I don't think even this ensemble would make Chad see me as anything but his little sister."

Nellie chuckles. "I beg to differ, my friend. But show me what you've got planned?"

I rush into my walk-in wardrobe, grabbing out my black denim ripped jeans, white crop tank and leather jacket with zips all over it. Yanking them on quickly, I admire myself in the cheval mirror, and I know it's the right outfit; sexy without revealing to much skin. Stopping back in front of my MacBook I turn, showing off to Nellie; who wolf whistles at me, laughing.

"Oh Roxy, damn girl!"

"You like?"

"Love, Roxy, fucking love. And Chad will too."

"I doubt that Nel, but thanks for the confidence."

"He'd have to be blind to not see you in this."

I laugh, clutching my bare stomach.

"Yeah, well, Chad is obviously blind. But I hope that maybe tonight might change things."

"Yeah me too, Roxy. Wish I could be there."

"Me too, Nel, but your parents anniversary dinner is more important."

"Yeah, speaking of, I gotta go help Nate organise some decorations. Go get your man, girl." She blows me a kiss.

"I'll try, Nel. Tell your parents congrats from me."

"Will do, bye Roxanne," she says, with a jeering tone.

I hang up, closing my MacBook and turning back to again admire myself in the cheval mirror.

I'm feeling confident, but also nervous as hell. I want Chad to see me as more than just Jessie's little sister. For him to have a bodily reaction in his daks like he does when he talks about or obviously thinks about Teagan.

I didn't tell him that I was actually awake the other morning when he got out of bed; didn't tell him that I felt his hard—and big—morning wood pressing against my butt. I'd desperately wanted to roll over and kiss him, to finally give him my v-card, considering I was wet but I didn't. Chad doesn't feel that way about me now, but I wonder if he once did and it makes a memory flash in my mind whilst I head to the bathroom to do my makeup.

Tears are streaming down my cheeks, and Chad grabs me by the shoulders, looking straight at me. "Rox, please don't cry. It's not forever. And I can still come over." "But your new family might not let you. And you've gotta go to a new school," I blurt out, then sob, hiccups rising up my throat. "Well, I'll make sure they let me Rox. You and Jessie are just as much my family as Carly is. I love you." A loud hiccup escapes my mouth, and I smile, "Really? You love me?" I know my words probably sound desperate, but I'm a thirteen-year-old girl with a huge crush on the guy standing in front of me. "Not like that, dufus," he says smirking at me.

"Oh well, then I um...I love you too, Chad," I say softly, but I most definitely mean it in 'that way'; the I want him to kiss me and do dirty things to me like I saw in the movie 'Fifty Shades of Grey' that Mum was watching one night.

He pulls me closer, brushing his thumb against my jaw, and I realise that my hiccups have stopped. His gaze is locked on mine, and butterflies explode in a flurry in my belly.

"Not goodbye, Rox, ok?" he says, almost stammering on the words, and making my heart pound. There's an odd promise in those words, and I take a deep breath in, exhaling a soft, "ok, Chad."

And before I can think, or take in other deep breath to calm myself, his delectable plump lips press

against mine in a soft sweet kiss;
my first kiss.

He pulls back and smiles. "That
was...wow...my...first...kiss," I
stammer, trying to hold back my
smile and also trying to hold back
from jumping up on my tiptoes to
kiss him again; harder.

"I know Rox. Save all your firsts for
me, please," he begs, smiling but
with a sad tone in his voice, "I gotta
go, ok?"

I take in a deep breath, not trusting
myself to say anything. My heart is
hammering in my chest, and I feel
like I'm about to melt when he
takes my hand, kissing it before he
pulls away. He doesn't look back
when he grabs his bags from beside
his feet and heads out the door to
his new foster family.

❤

That was the last time I'd seen Chad until he walked back into our lives a month ago. And applying my makeup now, thinking of that first kiss again sends the butterflies aflutter in my belly, and now also the tingles in my crotch. Tonight is definitely the night to make Chad see me like he did when I was thirteen. He loved me then, so maybe he still does.

16. *Chad*

*R*ox takes my hand, dragging
me inside 'Star sing Karaoke bar'.
She's giggling, on top of the world
and her outfit is hot as blazers.
My eyes don't know where to look,
her bare stomach, her cleavage or
across at Teagan—attached to
Jessie—who's wearing a figure-
hugging body con dress in red.

Teagan looks sexy, but it's an outfit that screams look at me and I totally get why Jessie is clinging onto her like a damn koala.

I'm jealous as fuck that I can't hold her in that dress and glancing around the bar when we enter I can see practically every guy in the room stops a moment to give her an approving glance.

"So birthday boy, what are you drinking tonight?" Rox asks me, pulling me up to the bar eagerly. Jessie, Teagan and the other mates I'd asked to come along go to find some seats across the room, near the stage where badly out of tune idiots are belting out a song I don't know.

"Beer, Rox. And you should get yourself a cocktail."

"Oh, I plan to get one of their famous frozen Strawberry Daiquiri's."

"Sounds sickly sweet, like you Rox." My words are meant to be a tease but she gives me dagger eyes. And I feel like a tool. "Sorry Rox."

"All good," she replies, before stepping up to the bar and ordering confidently.

Once the barman serves the drinks on a tray, I help her carry them over to the booth where our friends have sat.

We all sip the beers and cocktails, chatting amongst ourselves. My eyes watch Teagan sipping on the daiquiri, her lips wrapping around the straw and I wonder what they'd feel like around my cock instead of around a cocktail straw. I'm about to head up to the bar to order another round, noticing that Rox has finished her daiquiri, but she squeals loudly, "Oh my god, I love this song! Dance with me Teags?"

Teags? Since when are they so close.

"Oh yeah, Roxy. This song is my jam," Teagan yelps, getting to her feet. Rox pulls her onto the dance floor and they start dancing—gyrating—to 'Low by Flo Rida'. Their bodies are against each other, their arses swaying to the beat and Rox crouches to her knees when the words, *'she hit the floor, next thing you know, shorty got low, low'* come through the speakers. I'm watching them—with every other guy in the room—and my dick is screaming in my daks, throbbing and feeling like it's about to explode when Teagan slaps Rox's arse playfully like the words of the song say.

I can't fucking stand it, I need to get out there, and show them my moves. Sliding across the dance floor I wedge myself in between them and I'm a Chad sandwich between Rox and Teagan. Teagan is behind me, and Rox in front of me. They gyrate their hips against me, turning around and rubbing up and down all over me. It's so dirty and making me hot, sweaty and way too excited. I can see Jessie is angry and jealous, but I'm loving it too much to actually give a shit.

The song changes to something girly, and Rox giggles, another excited squeal comes from her lips, and her and Teagan start singing, *'Every time we touch'*. I'm still lost in the dancing when Jessie comes up to us, joining in by stepping up behind Teagan and pulling her away. Rox is still dancing against me, and I look at her, suddenly feeling completely mesmerised by her. The girl certainly knows how to dance and drive a guy crazy. She wraps an arm around my neck, her back still pressed against me. Her breathing has turned to panting, and our lips are mere centimetres from each other. I'm seriously considering kissing her—kissing Rox —but the song ends, and some other people step up onto to the stage for another karaoke round. Rox glares at me angrily before heading back to the bar. I officially feel like a complete wanker, and when I sit back down the angry glare Jessie gives me makes me feel even worse. Rox is not my girl—and neither is Teagan—so I don't know what his damn problem is; we were just dancing, but clearly he thinks something else is going on with me and his kid sister.

"Well, Chad? You wanna tell me something?"

"Nothing to tell."

"Really? So there's nothing going on between you and Roxanne?"

"Not a damn chance in hell, my friend. We were just dancing."

"Keep it that way, or you'll have no balls, my friend," he taunts menacingly.

Rox returns with some more drinks, and I down another beer in an attempt to get so drunk I don't have to remember my birthday going to shit and also maybe drunk enough to find a girl to take home to lose myself into for the night; to forget about girls who can't be mine.

17. Chad

*D*owning another beer, I feel it hit me hard, the buzz racing through my veins. The girls and Jessie are still killing it on the dance floor, but I'm taking a moment or two, to stand back from that madness; to give my aching dick a break. Although I'm not having much luck with that because Teagan and Rox are still all over each other and it's such a damn turn on.

But seeing Jessie latching onto Teagan is making me so jealous, so jealous that a stupid thought fills my mind and I know Jessie is going to think I'm a prick; a prick that can't stop cracking onto his girl but I want her to be mine.

Putting my pint down I saunter up to the stage, eyeing Teagan when I speak to the DJ about doing a karaoke number. He gives me an odd look when I choose Promiscuous by Timbaland & Nelly Furtado. "You sure mate? That's a duet."

"Dead sure, man," I reply, pointing to Teagan on the dance floor, "and I'm going to drag that pretty as fuck chick up to sing it with me."

"The brunette?" He enquires, licking his lips. I shake my head. "No, the blonde. The brunette might as well be my sister."

"Right, well the song's all lined up. Get ready."

I hear his words, watching as he lines up the karaoke track on the screen as the song he's playing fades out. Stepping up to the girls and Jessie, I grab Teagan's hand, leaning in to whisper in her ear, "Sing with me, Teags."

I'm trying to pull her up on the stage, only a metre from it when she snatches her hand from mine, screaming at me, "No Chad, please. I don't want to."

Her refusal is a kick in the guts. It shouldn't hurt so much but it feels like she's kneed me in the balls and when Jessie gives me dagger eyes I laugh. Yep, I fucking laugh, because

I'm the worst kinda friend and the least I can do now is jump on the stage and sing my broken heart out, whilst looking like a complete idiot.

I close my eyes, the song starting and I blurt out the rap words, *"How you doing, young lady?"*

I let my voice trail off, preparing myself for singing the female part. But I'm cut off when a sweet soprano—clearly a female— voice cuts through my ears. I open my eyes, feeling suddenly mesmerised by the voice, and gape at who is singing with me. I'm so lost and caught on the voice that I nearly miss my cue to sing the next male part.

Rox has jumped up on the stage and she's singing it with me.

I continue the male part, feeling the beat of the music rush through me, and also not able to take my eyes of Rox when she starts to dance around me, singing the words, *"Promiscuous boy, you already know I'm already yours."* I have to admit she looks fucking gorgeous strutting around the stage, completely owning the song, making the words hers. I feel the tension between us mounting—it's on fire—and I'm feeling hot, flustered and it's not just from the stage lights.

Roxanne Donaghey is teasing me, flaunting her hot as fuck body on the stage, singing her heart out to a dirty suggestive as hell song, and when she steps up right into my personal space; so close I can feel her breath over the microphone when she sings the final lines of the song.

The music starts to fade, and our breath is one—when we drop our microphones—our foreheads touching as we both pant from the rush of a karaoke duet; but also from the unmissable tension between us.

I don't know what the fuck just happened, but my dick is throbbing in my daks, and I want Rox right now. She grabs my hand, turning away from my intense gaze locked on hers and nodding towards the dance floor she pulls me away from the stage to what I'm sure is going to be both bliss and my doom.

18. Roxanne

Nodding towards my brother
still on the dance floor, I pull Chad
off the stage. He stumbles after me,
muttering something incoherent.
He's panting, breathless from
singing most likely as I'm sure it's

not from being so close to me we could have kissed.

He's begging me to slow down, but I'm practically sprinting and pulling him with me to get out of the club. Once outside the cold air hits me straight in the face and I inhale it, sucking in gulps to cool down my heated body. Dropping Chad's hand I turn to look at him, and the look on his face must mirror my own; completely and utterly confused.

"Um, Rox, what the hell just happened?" He asks, stepping into my personal space and pinning me against the wall. The streetlights cast a shadow over us and having him so close I notice the beginnings of a beard on his jawline, and damn does it make him look even sexier. Not able to meet his eyes that are staring at me like he's trying to see into my soul, I gaze down his body, taking in his outfit properly, noticing that our outfits are practically identical, except his white t-shirt is not a midriff exposing one.

And there's a definite turned on bulge at the front of his black jeans. He brings me back to reality, rubbing his thumb across my cheek and jaw. "Rox, seriously, tell me what just happened."

"I...sang...a...duet...with you...like...old times," I stammer, my words coming out between panting breaths.

"That wasn't like old times Rox." His voice sounds so husky, so sexy and it's sending pulses of pleasure through me.

"What do you mean? We always sang karaoke together."

"Yeah, but we sang Disney songs Rox, not..." he pauses, stepping back a little and running a hand through his ashen locks, flicking his unruly fringe back.

I swallow hard, trying not to hyperventilate from staring at him. Surely he knows the effect he has on me. "Not what Chad?" I ask with a hint of teasing.

"Not sexy as fuck songs like that Rox."

I scoff at him. He chose it, not me but I'm not stupid; I know he wanted to sing it with Teagan.

He doesn't see me that way.

"I get it Chad, you didn't want to sing it with me. But she's not your girl."

"I know that Rox, ok. And I didn't want to sing it with you, but I'm glad I did."

I gape at him, my mind racing with thoughts; dirty thoughts.

"Um, really?"

"Yeah Rox, seeing you up there and singing that with you...you looked damn hot."

"Um...thanks, so did you," I mutter, looking down at my feet.

"Rox, look at me, please," he pleads.

I gaze up at him again, feeling a blush rise up my cheeks.

"I wanna kiss you so bad right now, Rox," he confesses, again touching my cheek.

He leans in, and his lips are so close to mine, but before our lips meet I reach up to press a finger to his lips, whispering, "Not here."

Chad laughs, in that deep chuckling way that makes his chest vibrate. His hand reaches down between us, touching my crotch and he taunts, "So you want me to kiss you here, instead?"

A pulse of electricity courses through me. "Um...no...I meant like at home, not on a dirty street corner. I want our first kiss to be more private."

He chuckles again, taking my hand and dragging me to the curb, using his other hand to hail a taxi.

"It won't be our first kiss though Rox," he says, teasingly when a taxi pulls up in front of us.

Opening the door, he pulls me inside, giving the driver our address.

Leaning into my side, he whispers in my ear, "I haven't forgotten about you saving your firsts for me, Rox."

His words make my whole body tingle and my crotch damp. I want Chad so much, and right now it seems like he wants me to.

I'll probably regret it, but I'm going to give Chad the rest of my firsts that I've stupidly saved for him.

19. *Chad*

The whole taxi journey home I stare at Rox. It's clear her heart is pounding and she's affected by my presence. Leaning into her side, I whisper in her ear, "I haven't forgotten about you saving your firsts for me, Rox." She gulps, and blushes, shifting in her seat uncomfortably.

I don't know if she's honestly saved all her firsts for me—and I don't honestly care—but I'm as cliched as it is feeling a sudden attraction to her. It's like the original feelings I had for her as a horny teenager surfacing again. I knew then that I shouldn't have wanted her, but I always seem to want the girl I can't have—Teagan obviously—and Rox has also been the girl who can't be mine. But tonight my body—my dick—is screaming at me to throw caution to the wind and make Rox mine; to take her firsts and selfishly for some reason, I want to ruin her for whoever comes after me.

When the taxi pulls up in front of our house, I chuck the cabbie a fifty and grab Rox's hand the moment we're out of the taxi to pull her inside. She unlocks the door with her other hand, not letting go of my hand in hers. And as soon as we close the front door behind us, I'm dragging her down the hallway to my room.

Kicking the door closed I tug her into the room and press her body with mine against the wall.

Her chest is rising, falling, the outline of her tits visible.

Locking my eyes on hers, I ask softly, "You ok, Rox?"

"Um...yep," she gulps, "Just kiss me, please, Chad." I love how my name sounds on her lips, raspy and melodic. And without giving her warning I kiss her, hard.

And fuck me, kissing her—again—is something else. She moans against my mouth, her tongue teasing me

and I feel like I'm drowning in a Rox
fuelled lust pool.

Cupping her cheeks with my hands,
I tug her closer, taking her tongue
with mine to devour her mouth.
This kiss is fucking intense,
everything; and the best kiss of my
fucking life hands down. If I don't
pull away now, I'm going to cream
my daks from just a kiss, and that
never happens; ever.

Gasping I pull away, taking a deep
breath in whilst staring down at her
kissed red lips.

"Fuck Rox, that...fuck," I curse, still
drinking her in.

"Was it that good for you too?" she
asks, so fucking innocently my dick
hardens more.

I take a step back from her,
grabbing my dick through the front
of my jeans, nodding at her. "What
does it look like to you Rox?"

"Um, yes... I've never kissed anyone like that."

"Me either Rox. I nearly creamed my daks," I reply with a laugh.

Her eyes are looking me up and down, her lip between her teeth and I wonder what she's thinking. I know what I'm thinking and it's downright naughty, dirty as fuck and requires no clothes.

"You're just telling me that to fuck me," she mutters suddenly, stumbling on the words *'fuck me'*.

"Well, yeah, nah. I do want to fuck you Rox. But I want to give you all your firsts, remember?"

"But I've...I've done stuff."

"Mmm, like what Rox?" I tease, stepping closer to her again.

"Stuff," she replies, tugging me closer for another kiss, a kiss that sends lust pulsing through me. And breaking it again breathless, there's nothing more to say, but asking her, "Rox, can I touch your pussy?"

She bites down on her lip again and starts to strip for me, firstly shrugging off her leather jacket.

My dick is throbbing, getting excited as more of her body is exposed when she lifts her crop top over her head. She's wearing a black polka dot bra, and her tits practically spill out over the cups. Watching her doing the little strip tease—for me—is turning me on so bad.

Quickly to not miss the rest of the show, I yank my jacket and t-shirt off and focus back on Rox now shimmying out of her jeans; slowly tugging them down over her arse and down her sexy tanned thighs. And fuck me, she's wearing lacy black knickers that show her pussy is bare except for a landing strip.

"Fuck Rox, you're gorgeous."

She blushes, meekly replying, "Um, thanks. You're hot."

I laugh, yanking my jeans down awkwardly over my painfully hard dick before grabbing her around the waist. Her skin against my fingers feels incredibly soft and electric; it instantly heating at the contact.

Stepping backwards, I lure her towards the bed. And fall against it, bringing her down on top of me. Again I kiss her, revelling in the moans she makes that I'm sure are going to be my new favourite sound. I'm kicking myself for not getting naked with Roxanne before; the day I first saw her all grown up. Yeah, my dick didn't say hello looking at her—like it does with Teagan—but actually being with Rox is a mega turn on.

Breaking the kiss, I smirk at her.
"Rox, show me ya tits, please," I
beg with a teasing tone in my
voice.

"Promise to touch me if I do?"

"Oh yeah, baby," I taunt, smirking
again.

She sits up, reaching around her
back and undoing the clasp of her
bra. It falls off between us and I
grab it throwing it aside without
even looking. My eyes are staring
at her absolutely delectable, perky
and fucking glorious tits.

Licking my lips, I groan. "God, fuck,
Rox, your tits are fucking divine,
baby."

"Really?" she asks with that
innocent tone again. I wonder for a
moment about the tossers she's
supposedly been with before now.
They clearly were wankers, because

Roxanne has a body fit for sin and I'm about to go to hell.

I don't answer her, just sit up more, leaning forward to grab her around the waist. And teasingly I lick across one of her hard nipples.

The moan that escapes her lips is loud and lascivious. I give the other nipple the same sweet torture, swirling my tongue over her skin.

"Chad, more, more, please," she begs, panting.

Again I pull her down for a kiss, a hot dirty kiss that's tongues and teeth clashing in a battle of dominance.

I'm so turned on, but I want to make her scream my name first, want to make her moan from my hands on her.

Still kissing her I slide a hand between us, running a finger over her clit through the lace.

Her hips buck and she moans against my lips, biting my bottom lip. "Mmm, please, please touch me," she whispers breaking the kiss.

"You want me to make you come, Rox?"

"Yes...yes...please," she pleads, her tone raspy.

Watching her I slip my hand into her knickers and flick my thumb over her clit.

"Oh," she moans, closing her eyes. I slip a finger inside her wet as pussy, curling it up to her sweet spot. She starts panting, moaning and rocking her hips. "Feel good, baby?" I ask, teasingly and whilst inserting another finger.

"A...a...amazing," she says huskily through her moans. I thrust my fingers in and out of her pussy, loving how wet and how deliciously tight she is.

She rocks her hips on my fingers harder, and when I rub my thumb over her clit again she trembles, her whole body shaking from her climax, and she calls out, "Oh fuck, fuck Chad!"

I withdraw my fingers, putting them up to her lips when she collapses against my chest.

Her tongue darts out between her lips to lick them and the lascivious moan escapes her mouth again.

"One first," she mutters, softly.

"And that was?"

"Tasting my own come," she says laughing sweetly.

"I want to taste you, Rox," I muse, smirking at her. She giggles, kissing me and I can taste a hint of her musky sweet nectar on my tongue. And fuck, I want more; want to lick her pussy until she explodes all over my face.

"Sounds like a dirty first."

Oh, god, she did not just say that.

Grabbing her I pick her up and put her down on the bed, kissing her again before trailing kisses over her tits again, and down her perfect flat tanned stomach, licking over her scar. She bucks her hips up.

Her body is so gorgeous. Reaching her lacy knickers, I kiss her clit through the fabric and she lets out a loud scream of pleasure but then gasps in horror. "Chad, stop. Did you hear that?"

"Hear what?"

"Jessie and Teagan coming home."

"So?" They'll just stumble into his room," I tell her, stretching over her to kiss her again.

"Maybe, but what if Jessie checks on me. To make sure I got home ok?"

"He won't, stop worrying," I reply unconvincingly.

She doesn't reply, just shifts on the bed and gets up, picking up all her clothes and sneaking out of my room; without another word.

She doesn't even look back at me, and that's how I know despite how it felt being with Rox was a bad idea. She's not my girl, but a part of me wants her to be because I've never felt anything like I did when kissing her. And thinking about her in the room next door I grab my still hard dick, stroking it and coming in my boxers in less than a minute.

Yep, I'm fucked.

20. Roxanne

Sitting on Nellie's bed I'm trying not to cry. Next to me, she's sitting cross-legged, rubbing my back in comfort.

"Roxy, it can't have been that bad."

"It wasn't bad. So far from bad, but I...I shouldn't have gone that far with him."

I look at my best friend then, worrying my lip between my teeth.

"You told me you didn't sleep with him?"

Pulling back from her I clutch my knees to my chest. "I didn't, we kissed, and he fingered me. And Nel, it was amazing."

"So what happened? Why didn't you go for the home run and give him your v-card?"

Pouting, I reply a little angrily, "Jessie came home. And I panicked."

"Shit, well, I kinda get you now, but honestly why does Jessie even care?"

"Because Chad's his best friend, dufus. He doesn't want him to take advantage of me."

"I don't think that's the case, is it?"

"To be honest, I don't know. But I feel like he used me, said things to me to make me feel like he had the same reaction to being together that I did."

"You should talk to him, Roxy. He might surprise you."

"Yeah, no thanks. I'm just going to avoid him until he forgets it ever happened."

"Suit yourself. So are you staying tonight?"

"Yeah, if that's ok. Easier to not face him if I'm not home."

She laughs, getting up off the bed to get out some PJs for me to wear. Throwing them at me she jeers, "You're a dufus, Roxy."

Once we're both in our PJs and lying under the covers Nellie sighs and asks me softly, "Would you have fucked him if Jessie didn't come home?"

"Yeah," I let out with a moan.

"You should make it happen, Roxy. You can't stay a virgin forever waiting for Chad to make the move."

Playfully I punch her in the side. "Just because you lost yours on your sixteenth birthday to daggy Rick Hickman doesn't give you the right to make me feel like a prude, Nel."

"Yeah, worse decision ever. I wish I'd waited; not til I found the one, but at least until a better one."

"Yeah," I muse softly, thoughts of Chad being my one filling my mind. He'd always been mine, even before our first kiss, even before the other night.

❤

It's the middle of the night, but I'm not scared when I hear my bedroom door creak open and footsteps coming into my room. He often comes in during the night, after he's had a nightmare about his parents' death. Stepping closer to my king single bed, he whispers into the darkness, "Rox, you awake?"

"Yeah," I whisper back, feeling the bed dip with his weight. I scoot over, closer to the wall and pull the covers back. He climbs in next to me, and I drape an arm over his body.

I try not to notice how warm his skin feels under his t-shirt and try not to think about what happened a few nights ago when he sang the karaoke song.

I can hear his sobs lingering in the air. "Did you dream about them again?" I ask softly, gazing down at him.

He looks across at me, his plump lip between his teeth for a moment before he mutters softly, "No, it was me Rox. I...I...died in the crash and they weren't even at my funeral."

"Oh Chad, I'm sorry. It was just a nightmare."

"It should have been me Rox. I took my sister's parents away."

I gape at him, and he clears his throat before clarifying, "They were coming home early for my stupid science competition."

"Chad, you can't still blame yourself for their death. I don't know much about grief and stuff but Carly needs you to be her big brother more than ever."

"I know, Rox. Thanks for being a good little sister too." He laughs then, pulling back from me a little,

and nearly falling off the edge of the bed.

Grabbing him harder around the waist I pull him closer, and he laughs again, grabbing me around the waist at the same time. He starts to tickle me and wiggling in his arms I giggle, mumbling, "Stop Chad, stop."

His tickling stops, and he looks at me with an odd look in his eyes.

I don't know what it is, but when my hand brushes against his body under the sheets accidentally I'm sure his dick is hard. And that can only mean he liked touching me; as much as I enjoyed the tickling, even though I protested.

He takes a deep breath in, sighing, and closing his eyes, murmuring, "You save me, Rox. You're mine, my saviour."

*Rolling over, I accept his arms
around me when he pulls me closer,
and murmur, "You're mine, Chad."*

❤

That memory hits me hard in the
chest, making my heart pound and
I gasp for air. "Roxy, shit, are you
ok?"

"Yeah, I'm fine. I...um just
remembered something about
Chad."

"Ooo do tell."

"It's nothing. Just something he
said to me when we were kids."
I shrug, hoping she won't probe me
for more, because disclosing that
memory to Nellie—even though
she's my best friend—feels too
intimate.

I need to talk to Chad, but I'm not
ready to face him, or my feelings.

Nellie rolls over. "Oh ok, fair enough. Goodnight."

"Goodnight, Nel," I reply closing my eyes.

Chad's face just before he kissed me surfaces in my mind and drifting to sleep I think of our night together, hoping that it won't be the last.

21. *Chad*

*E*ver since the night with Rox, that I've honestly not been able to get off my mind she's been avoiding me. And when she has been around, she won't look at me, let alone talk to me about what happened.

I admit I was a prick in the moment, but I want to tell her that being with her—really being with her—blew me away. The feelings I experienced when kissing her—and touching her—were new to me, and I acted like a prick, acted nonchalant because they scared me, bringing back all the feelings I had for her as a teenager. I fought those feelings then because I thought having feelings for my best mates little sister was wrong; she was like a sister to me but now as a grown man things have changed. I'm more than pissed off with Rox because she won't talk to me. I need to explain and clear the air; get rid of the tension that's descended on the household.

After getting up and draining my snake quickly in the bathroom, I head to the kitchen opening up the cupboard to search for some cereal to eat. There's not much choice, cornflakes or Nutri-Grain. I decide on the Nutri-Grain; opening the packet and eating them straight from the box whilst leaning against the bench.

Jessie walks into the kitchen and gives me an odd look noticing my off—weird—behaviour.

"Morning, Chadster."

"Morning Jessman," I reply, nearly choking on a piece of Nutri-Grain.

"Why have you been acting so weird lately?" he questions me, grabbing a bowl and tipping cornflakes into it.

"No reason, just feeling like the vibes here are off at the moment."

"What the fucks that mean?"

Putting the Nutri-Grain down I gulp. "Rox isn't talking to me. And isn't here half the time. And when she is she's a grump."

"Have Roxanne's bad moods got anything to do with you? You both left early from your birthday drinks."

Again I gulp, swallowing down the lump in my throat, trying to get some saliva into my dry mouth.

"Um, yeah we did, but I just wanted her to get home safe. She was tanked."

"So nothing happened? You just came home together?"

I nod. "Yep, that's it. That's all. Nothing happened between us, I promise."

He raises his eyebrows at me; his tell that he doesn't believe me, but he doesn't push the subject, so I ask, "How're things with Teagan?"

He chuckles then, his hand slipping a little when pouring the milk on his cornflakes. "Good man, thanks for keeping your mitts off. But you really should get ya self a girl."

"Yeah, I know man. My hand isn't doing it for me," I reply laughing.

He laughs with me for a moment and my mind wanders to thinking about Teagan. As if talking and thinking about her has summoned her she happens to walk into the house at that moment; unlocking the front door with her own key. Walking into the kitchen she gives me an odd look that I can't decipher. It seems like she's wishing me away, but also it's a touch flirtatious when she kisses Jessie and looks at me out of the corner of her eyes.

A month ago—a week ago even— her looking at me whilst kissing Jessie would have turned me on, but now I'm actually kinda repulsed.

"Do you mind getting a room?" I hiss at them.

She laughs breaking her kiss with Jessie, and locks her eyes on me, trying to eye fuck me when she trills, "Sorry Chad, I just can't help it when I'm around this one." She giggles, playfully punching Jessie in the side.

"Yeah, whatever," I reply walking back to my room.

I stop by Rox's door to listen—to see—if she's home, but it's clear she's not when Bruno comes bounding out of Jessie's room instead; and I know I've clearly lost the plot when I pat his fur and consider telling him I'm in love— yep, in love—with his pretty owner.

22. Roxanne

Coming home from Nellie's I feel like an intruder, sneaking into my own house so I don't wake anyone—and by anyone—I specifically mean Chad. I know I need to talk to him, but I'm scared that he'll just shatter my heart.

Tiptoeing into the house, after
closing the front door behind me
I'm heading down the hallway
when I see the glow from the fridge
light.

I stop dead, fixated on him bent
over and staring into the fridge.
He's only wearing super tight red
boxers, and they outline his
gorgeous butt.

My mouth is watering, and for a
moment I want to rush over to him
and push him against the fridge,
taking his mouth to mine in a kiss.
Kissing him is all I've thought
about, his kiss is ingrained in my
mind, and I can still feel his kisses
against my lip like a bruise. And
that is also why kissing him again,
when I'm still angry, upset that he
used me and didn't obviously have
the same reaction to the
experience is a very bad idea.

He suddenly shifts, stepping back from the fridge with a bottle of water in his hand. He squeezes it, and without turning around he says, "Hey Rox."

Panicking I gulp, wondering if I should say anything or just walk away. I've done so well at avoiding him, avoiding the no doubt awkward conversation we need to have, that I don't want to have because it will make it real.

It will shatter my heart even more than it already is.

Still, I can't get my feet to cooperate, and he comes over to me, sipping on his water with a cocky grin on his face; that, of course, shows off his double dimple.

"We need to talk Rox."

"No. We. Don't," I mutter, biting down on my lip, and sliding back from him when he enters my personal space.

My whole body hums with him so close again. My converse sneakers squeak on the tiles when I step back and watching Chad take another big gulp of his water I let out a squeak from my lips. He laughs, that laugh that makes his chest vibrate and his muscles ripple.

"Rox, please. Just let me explain."

I huff at him, folding my arms over my chest. "There's nothing to explain, Chad."

I turn to walk away, not wanting to look at his face showing fake sincerity.

The only thing that I can do is avoid him because even just being in the same room as him hurts too much.

I can't have Chad, partly because he doesn't want me as much as I want him, but mostly because he's my brothers best friend, and he might as well be my brother. I don't want to think of him as my brother, but thinking about him that way is the only way I can stop myself from thinking about kissing him, and about how his touch made me feel.

It's no use though; my head knows he's not my brother, and my heart is his. I love Chad, I've always loved Chad, even before I knew what love was, and he'll never love me back.

23. *Chad*

*A*fter having barely slept, for thinking of Rox all night I'm feeling incredibly tired and frustrated because she's still avoiding me and won't even entertain a conversation with me. Waking up my head is pounding, and there's music blaring from the lounge room.

Getting out of bed, I pick up a t-shirt, yanking it over my head whilst I'm stumbling out of my bedroom.

Heading to the source of the noise —clutching my morning wood—I find Teagan is dancing around the house, cleaning whilst she's singing.

"Teagan," I call out, "can you turn it down?"

She dances over to me, her eyes darting down to my dick. And she licks her lips. I ignore the flirtatious gesture and ask, "Your music...can you turn it down?"

"Yeah, Jessie's out for a run."

"Ok, I um didn't ask that."

"Yep, ok," she says, sashaying away from me.

I head back to my bedroom, slamming the door and flopping down on the bed, pulling the pillow over my head. My dick is still hard, but seeing Teagan dancing around wearing some short arse nightie had no effect on it this time. I can't doubt that she's still gorgeous, but I don't want Jessie's girl now.

My mind wanders to the girl my heart wants—that my body now wants—and my morning wood throbs remembering her kisses and how her tight perfect body responded to my touch.

Sliding my hand into my boxers, I fist my dick, about to start wanking when my bedroom door cracks open and someone tiptoes into my room. Having my eyes closed I'm hoping it's Rox, but I don't dare open my eyes.

"Want some help?" a soft voice asks. It doesn't sound like Rox, but I don't open my eyes and mumble, "Um, no, um yes."

She comes further into the room, diving at the bed. I still have my hand on my dick and she lets out an appreciative hum before she kisses me, but I don't feel anything —nothing, nada—my dick isn't throbbing, my lips not on fire like they were when I kissed Rox.

She starts to touch me, her hands sliding between us and gripping my dick—hard—and I know it's not Rox.

Opening my eyes I push Teagan away, off my lap. And my eyes immediately focus on the door where Jessie has come stumbling in screaming, "What the fuck Chad?"

I jump out of bed, grabbing the sheets and holding them against my junk whilst I stumble towards my best mate.

"Nothing happened man."

He balls his fists. "As if I'm going to fucking believe you, when you're naked with my girlfriend on top of you."

Teagan takes that opportunity to stand up, glancing between Jessie and me for a moment, before she steps up close to him, pressing her hands into his chest. "Jess, it was me. I um…I kissed him, but that's it."

His pupils dilate, and he clenches and unclenches his fists, before caressing her cheek softly.

"Whatever, Teags baby, please just meet me in my room. We'll talk about this in private."

She walks out and Jessie turns his attention to me. I have no idea what to say, but I haven't done anything wrong.

She kissed me, and I thought she was Rox. But she's not Rox, and I can't say that to Jessie either. He can't know I kissed, touched his little sister and that I'm in love with her. He won't care that Rox is mine, won't care that I love her, but that I took advantage of her.

I'm about to open my mouth to try and say something, but he interrupts me, yelling, "You…you…I can't Chad." He's seething again, clenching his fists again when he hurls more angry words at me, "Just pack your shit and get the fuck out of my house."

He's furious, and stomping out he slams his bedroom door behind him.

I can hear him yelling with Teagan when I head to the bathroom to have a quick shower before packing up my things.

I'm screwed, nowhere to go except home with my tail between my legs.

24. *Chad*

*A*fter my shower, I'm haphazardly throwing my clothes in my gym bag. Jessie and Teagan clearly made up, because moans and screams of pleasure have been coming from his room for the past half hour; and it's making my stomach churn.

But it's also the fact that I'm leaving
Rox before I can really be with her,
and tell her that I'm in love with
her. It's not like she'd believe me
because she'll think like last time I
told her I love her that I mean it like
a brother, and I don't.

I'm in love with Roxanne Donaghey,
and again, I'm being forced to walk
away.

I yank on my black jeans—that I
wore that night—and shove my
arms into my leather jacket. There
are tears stinging my eyes, and I
sniff them back, slinging my gym
bag over my shoulder and grabbing
my surfboard, tucking it under my
arm.

Walking out of the bedroom, I
creep past Rox's room, and her
door is open. She's sitting on her
bed, knees up with her laptop
resting on it. Her hair is down, in

ringlets around her face and she looks so fucking beautiful; my breath hitches.

I shouldn't be standing there staring at her, contemplating saying goodbye, but I can't move. Part of me just wants to walk away, to let her be and let her go.

But I also want to drop my stuff on the floor, and rush into her room to dive at the bed and kiss her senseless.

I'm about to do just that—curse Jessie finding out—when Bruno spots me, rushing out and bowling me over; giving me sloppy doggy kisses.

"I'm going to miss you to, buddy," I tell him, ruffling his furry head.

"Bruno, stop," Rox calls out, getting up off the bed, and striding over towards her bedroom door.

She's only wearing boyshort
knickers and a tight t-shirt; that
show off her sexy curves.
Fuck she's gorgeous. And mine. No,
Not mine.

She glares at my bag—and
surfboard—and sniffs back a sob.
"Why do you have a bag? Are you
leaving?"
"Yeah, I am. Jessie kicked me out
because Teagan kissed me."
"You kissed Teagan?" she says,
sighing and looking at the floor.
"I...did...but."
"Seriously Chad, how could you?
After we?"
I gaze over her body, watching her
reaction to my words. And I can tell
her heart is broken, so even though
I don't mean the harsh words I say
them anyway, "Why do you care
Rox? You're not my girl."

Her mouth drops open, but no words come out and I pick up my bag—and surfboard—again, trudging out without another word.

I'm broken, shattered, again, having walked out on the only girl I've ever loved. I said she's not my girl, but she always will be my girl.

Closing the front door behind me, and heading home I can only hope that letting her go is the right thing to do. Because just thinking about Roxanne not being my girl is absolute hell.

To be continued...

Australian Slang Glossary

Ute-Truck

Bludger- someone lazy, doesn't do much and possibly relies on social security benefits

Ripper- something really good/great

Ridgy-Didge- Cool

Bonzer-Great, awesome

Pash/ing/ed- to kiss/make out

Arvo- afternoon

Chunder- Vomit, throw up

Gobby- Blowjob

Aussie Kiss- going down on a girl

Daks- pants/trousers/underwear

Undies/Knickers/Jocks-underwear (female knickers, male Jocks, undies both)

Dakking/ed- to pull or have pulled someone daks down (see above)

Bathers- universal name for female swimwear

Budgie Smugglers- small male swimmer that looks like underwear (google this one to see)

Thongs- Footwear, otherwise known as flip flops

Esky- Cooler-you keep drinks cool in it

Dunny- toilet

Bogan-white trash/trailer trash

Old Fella- Your father/Dad

Franger- Condom, Trojan etc

Milo- a malt chocolate powered drink mix (can be made hot or cold)

Macca's-MacDonalds

Fair Dinkum- used to emphasise or seek confirmation of the genuineness or truth of something

Fucking/Bloody oath- similar to above, but an extreme or emphasised way of saying yes.

Shark Week/Rags- A woman's monthly cycle

Stuffed if I know- a nicer way to say fucked if I know

AFL- Australian Rules Football

Playlist

Below is the playlist of songs for this story.
The Spotify playlist link is at the bottom.

1. Jessie's Girl-Rick Springfield
2. Real Feels-RITUAL, Denzel Curry
3. Promiscuous-Nelly Furtado, Timbaland
4. A whole new world-original Aladdin soundtrack
5. Kiss the Girl-The Little Mermaid soundtrack
6. I Want You to Want Me-Letters to Cleo
7. Time after time-Quietdrive
8. Low-Flo Rida, T-Pain
9. Everytime We Touch-Cascada
10. On without you-Incubus

About the Author

Caz May is a librarian/teacher by trade, but was always destined to be an author from a young age.

In her spare time, she can be found devouring books or writing her own stories with characters that may not be the typical romance heroes but are loveable just as much.

Caz is married to her own real-life bearded hero and has two fur babies.

She lives for Iced coffee, especially from Gloria Jeans or a Farmers Union but pretty much just loves food in general.

When she's not writing, or reading a book most likely she can probably be found asleep or binge-watching shows on Netflix and Stan. And probably also drooling over her character inspiration on Instagram as well.

Check out her Instagram or other socials to get in touch.

Instagram- @cazmayauthor

Facebook- @CazMayAuthor

BookBub-Caz May https://www.bookbub.com/profile/caz-may

Spotify- cazcat25

Website- https://cazcat25.wixsite.com/cazmay-author

Wattpad- https://www.wattpad.com/user/Caz-May

Acknowledgments

Hey lovely readers!
I can't believe another book is done. I've really enjoyed writing this one, and honestly there is only a couple of acknowledgments that need to be said for this book.

Firstly, my best friend Bianca, who from the very start of writing this book has constantly encouraged me to keep writing all the crazy ideas that come into my head. She's a huge music fan, and I think that's another reason why she encouraged me so much with this story.

Secondly, I need to thank my Bookstagram buddy, Amanda (@amanda.loves.books) She's always willing to listen to my crazy ideas and is always excited to read my stories. And this time around I'm giving her a special shoutout for helping me choose the song for the karaoke scene and I love how that chapter turned out.

And lastly, as always my amazing husband who constantly encourages me. He helped me decide on the right text and perfect placement for the cover and I love how that turned out. He is my forever.

I should probably also mention my fur babies, Enzo my Chihuahua and Rosie my tabby cat. They give me lots of late night cuddles when I'm writing and that makes getting through writing a book a lot easier.

Signing off! For now!

Not my Girl
Caz May xx

CPSIA information can be obtained
at www.ICGtesting.com
Printed in the USA
BVHW031354210520
580082BV00001B/92

9 780648 853404